Waste Deep

Brock Eastman

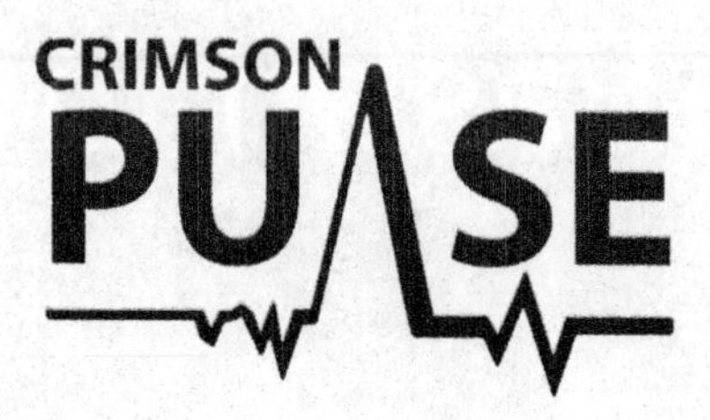

Unless otherwise identified, Scripture quotations are taken from the King James Version.

This story first appeared in Clubhouse Magazine in July 2016.

Illustrations used under license and permission from David Miles

ISBN: 978-1-946692-00-9 (pbk)

For Worldwide Distribution, Printed in the U.S.A.

1 2 3 4 5 6 7 8 9 10

Dedication

Uncle Douglas,

When I was given this assignment for Clubhouse Magazine, the theme was: Humility (John 13:14.) Immediately you popped into my head. I've always known you to put others first and do what you could to serve them, your humble spirit (aside from when you and dad are teasing each other) is always evident. Seeing how you serve others while being in Waste Management was the perfect inspiration for the Wikk family's story in their undersea colony. And the science and technology behind your job provided a great real-world example for Waste Deep.

ACKNOWLEDGEMENTS

My wife, **Ashley:** I am thankful every day for you and the wonderful life we have with our beautiful children. With you, at my side, I have the courage to try anything.

My **Kinley**: You read more books than any kid I know. I love your hunger to learn.

My **Elsie**: You are so creative and talented. It's fun to watch you dance and act and sing!

My **Waverly**: Your imagination is alive. Sneaking up to watch you pretend with your toys is inspirational to my imagination.

My **Declan**: Stay little. You're growing up so quick, and you are so inquisitive.

Contents

1 – Fresh Start

Grey Wikk pulled a pulsonic rake across the surface of the sludge pool. The room filled with a distinct odor, like a mixture of manure and vinegar.

Once you got past the smell and into the science, the sludge pool was fascinating. Sea worms called Nemertea and bacteria worked around the clock to break down waste. The Nemertea were the most exciting, though, all sorts of colors and patterns; orange, yellow, red, and green. Grey's dad told him that one specimen had grown to nearly 200 ft. in length.

On the other side of the lab, Grey's mom sprayed treated sewage water onto her garden. Grey could see the sprouts peeking out from the hydroponic pools. Before long, the crew of the Antarctic Research Colony would feast on fresh vegetables.

The underwater base was located far below the Ross Ice Shelf in the Southern Ocean. Ultra-frigid temperatures made for a unique laboratory environment. Most humans had never seen these aquatic life forms before.

The research colony provided access to unique life forms no human would otherwise observe. Research on fish and other creatures already resulted in new medicines and exciting technological advances, like Lumiskyn, which in Grey's opinion was awesome. His parents had made him a pair of gloves made from the organic luminescent material.

Living deep in the ocean was matchless; a rare opportunity for most, and that was not lost on Grey. The alien world of the seafloor intrigued him as nothing else had. What new discoveries were out there waiting?

If only he were old enough to take one of the mini-subs for a swim or even take the ice lift to the surface.

Grey and his parents had arrived three months ago via a much larger submarine. The kind that didn't have to surface for more than a year, and dive to the lowest depths of the oceans.

Grey's parents were scientists; experts at reclamation, harvest and decomposition.

The kids at Grey's school had a simpler name for the Wikks: "the garbage family."

But Grey knew why he was there, and he knew why his parents had chosen this field of specialty.

The world above the waves was failing, and the Wikks were part of an effort to find ways to save the Earth or discover ways for humans to live beneath the waves. The pollution of the ocean had led to entire species of sea life dying off, including oxygen creating algae. And atmospheric pollution had led to rising air temperatures and melting ice caps and thereby rising sea levels. Drought and famine followed. And soon after wars over water and food.

Three dozen underwater bases were constructed across the world to begin testing if indeed humans could live beneath the waves and survive, while also devising ways to restore the oceans. The Wikks were focused on the latter goal.

2 – Cleaning Crew

"Call the scout team!" Grey's dad shouted. "It's time for inspection."

Grey smiled. He whistled a short tune into the m-Com on his wrist.

A minute later, three penguins leaped out of the access pool. Waves, Mae Mae and Grace had been trained to retrieve samples from the ocean. Grey opened the pack strapped to Mae Mae's chest and sorted the fish and krill into several holding tanks.

"Mae Mae brought back an icefish," Grey said, holding up the sample.

"That's an excellent sign," Mom said. "With the algae population on the rise and the bottom-feeders returning, we'll soon have a sustainable habitat."

"I picked up a blue whale on sonar today," Grey's dad said, washing his hands with gritty orange soap.

"This calls for a celebration," Grey said. "Who wants a treat?"

The Penguins flapped their wings and waddled toward him, chattering loudly. Grey tossed feeder fish into their beaks.

"I'm so thankful God called us here," Mom said, wiping the dirt off her face.

Grey didn't completely understand how anyone could be *called* to waste management. But the longer he watched his parents work, the more he appreciated it. Each day they made the oceans a little cleaner and took care of the other colonists. They waded knee-deep in the muck so everyone else didn't have to.

Waves waddled over to the sludge pool and flicked a smelly green glob at Grey.

Mom laughed. "You'd better go shower." She looked at the m-Com on her wrist. "School start in 15 minutes."

Grey sighed. *School.* And though his family had been assigned to save the world, he still had to attend school, but so did the other kids. The base was more like a colony, just on a smaller scale. More than a thousand people called the base home. Most were scientists; a few were military.

Grey took his pack and waved bye to his parents, then headed into the long corridor that connected the laboratory to the rest of the base.

3 – Garbage Kid

Grey walked the corridor leading from the Waste Reclamation center back toward a nexus that attached to the Wikk's habitation pod and a stairwell. The Waste Reclamation Center sat on the ocean floor and thereby was the lowest level of the base, which was also where his family's habitation pod was. It made it easy for his parents to access their lab and do their work, but it made him feel like a lower class citizen.

He was halfway along the corridor, which meant six more hatches. Like every section of the base, it was broken up into airtight compartments to protect against flooding. But the extra safety took more time. He had to press each keypad and wait for each hatch to spiral open.

When he opened the second hatch, to his shock, three kids from school whispered nearby in a huddle.

"What are you doing here?" Grey asked.

Lloyd and Miranda stared at the floor. Hamlin snickered. "We're betting who can hold their breath the longest," he said. Grey knew there was more to it than that.

Hamlin sniffed the air daintily. "Something smells awful. Oh wait, that's you."

The other kids laughed.

Grey blushed. He'd been teased before about his parents' work. It was the same at the last four stations his family had been assigned. Each time he hoped for a new start, only to be disappointed. "They're just ignorant," his dad would say. "Show them the science."

Grey forced himself to smile. "Do you want to meet the penguins?" he asked.

"You work with penguins?" Miranda asked, suddenly excited.

"They probably smell worse than he does," Hamlin said.

Grey shrugged. *So much for science.* He squeezed past Hamlin and walked toward the living quarters to change clothes. The others followed him, laughing at the slimy footprints he left behind.

"You're leaving tracks, Garbage Kid," Hamlin teased.

Grey did his best to ignore them. Midway through the corridor, the ground began to shake. Grey braced himself against the curved wall.

"What was that?" Lloyd asked.

"Some kind of collision," Grey said. "Maybe a mini-sub swept off course."

"Let's get out of here," Miranda said.

A loud bang echoed above them. The corridor shook violently. Grey was thrown to the ground. It wasn't until the shaking stopped that he could hear a faint hissing sound.

The tunnel was leaking.

4 – Hold Your Breath

Seawater sprayed into the corridor. Orange hazard lights blinked on and off. The hatches on either side of them swirled closed with a hiss and click.

The safety system must be isolating the damage, Grey realized. "Quick, this way!" he shouted.

"I'm not going to the sewers," Hamlin said. He turned and tried the hatch leading back toward the rest of the base. "It's locked."

"Safety system has kicked in to protect the colony," Grey said.

"He's right," Lloyd said. His dad worked with the safety team that designed safety protocols and monitored the base.

The four kids scrambled toward the waste management chamber. Hamlin tugged at the hatch, but it wouldn't budge.

"We're trapped!" Lloyd screeched.

The roof groaned as a second leak burst over their heads spraying icy water into the section or tube.

Miranda screamed.

Grey pulled up his m-Com and called his mom.

"Are you okay?" Mom asked.

"Yes and no," Grey answered. "Nobody was injured, but the corridor is flooding, and all the exits are sealed."

"Who else is with you?" she asked in surprise.

"Three kids from school," Grey said.

"Stay close to the hatch," Mom said. "Something hit the station. Dad's calling Rescue Patrol."

"They'd better hurry up!" Grey said.

The water puddled an inch deep at his feet. Aside from drowning, the next danger would be hypothermia if they were stuck in the frigid water too long. He wore rubberized boots, but his classmates wore simple cloth shoes.

Lloyd hugged Miranda tightly, more for his sake than hers.

Hamlin pressed his body against the wall, trying to keep both feet off the ground. He slipped and landed hard on the metal floor. "Oww!" he grunted, clutching his arm.

The longest minute of Grey's life ticked by as the water rose to his ankles.

"Grey." His mom's voice sounded strained. "Listen carefully. The colony has suffered significant structural damage. Rescue Patrol cannot reach you in time, and the submarine bay is flooded."

Miranda and Lloyd gasped. Grey's skin prickled. He rubbed his head, smearing green goo onto his face. He coughed, having forgotten about the penguin's gift to him as he departed the laboratory.

The putrid smell gave him an idea.

"Mom," Grey said, "does the sewer line run parallel to this corridor?"

His mom gasped. "Yes, it does!"

"Can you flush the pipe from there?" Grey asked.

"Yes," his mom said. "Great thinking. It could be your way out."

"What are you talking about?" Hamlin grumbled. "I'm not going in a sewer pipe!"

"The pipe empties into a sludge pool in my parents' lab," Grey explained. "We can access the pipe from a maintenance panel halfway down the corridor."

Hamlin turned a pale green, but he didn't say a word. The water had reached their shins.

This was no time to be picky.

5 – Tunnel Vision

The sewer line ran along the floor of the corridor. The kids ran to an access hatch. Lloyd and Grey pulled the lever with all their might.

"It's stuck," Grey said. "Help us." Miranda joined in, but not Hamlin. They pressed and pulled hard.

Thwunk! The hatch groaned as it opened. The stench in the sewer pipe filled the corridor.

"Yuck! That's worse than anything I've ever smelled," Lloyd gasped.

"I'm not going in there," Miranda said.

"It's our best option," Grey said. "The water's getting deeper every moment."

Lloyd nodded then climbed headfirst into the pipe. Miranda followed. When it was Hamlin's turn, he shook his head.

"I can't do it," Hamlin said, gritting his teeth.

"Don't be stubborn," Grey replied. "You can handle the smell for two minutes."

"You don't understand," Hamlin said. "I think I broke my arm when I fell. There's no way I can pull myself through the pipe."

"Is everything okay, Grey?" his mom asked over the m-Com. "Your friends made it to the lab, but we're still waiting for you."

"Hamlin can't use his arm to crawl through the pipe," Grey explained.

"He has to try," Mom said. "You two can't stay there you could get hypothermia or drown.

Grey tried to think. The water was up to his knees. If the sewer pipe flooded, they wouldn't be able to get through anymore; their only escape would be gone.

"God, I don't know what to do," he prayed. "Please show me how to save Hamlin."

Over the m-Com, Grey heard a noisy squawk.

"Are the penguins with you?" he asked his mom.

"Yes," she replied.

"Tie a rope to Grace's pack. When she answers my signal, I'll put the pack on Hamlin, and you can help pull him to safety."

"Great idea," his mom said.

Grey poked his head into the sewer pipe and whistled the penguin's tune. Then he waited.

Seconds later, a black and white head popped out of the sewer pipe.

"Good girl," Grey whispered.

6 – Saved by Grace

Inch by inch, they tugged Hamlin through the sewer. As Grey crawled close behind, he heard the bully whimper.

"That must really hurt," Grey said.

"The arm's bad," Hamlin admitted. "But the claustrophobia's much worse."

"Wow," Grey said. "If you hate tight spaces, it must be tough to live in a place like this."

Hamlin grunted in agreement. "Why are you so kind to me?" he asked.

"I couldn't let you drowned," Grey said.

"Yeah, but you were nice before this. Even when I make fun of you, you don't fight back."

Grey thought about his parents. "God calls us to help in strange ways," he said. "Whether it's studying yucky sludge or helping people who treat us like garbage; no job is too messy when we do it for Him."

Grace wiggled ahead of them, calling back and forth to Mae Mae in the lab. A nasty brownish-yellow slime stuck to the inside of the pipe. Grey didn't want to think about what it could be.

Suddenly his knees felt wet.

"Hurry!" Grey shouted. "The water's coming in."

Hamlin started to gasp as panic set in.

"It's going to be okay," Grey assured him. "You're almost there."

The boys spilled out of the pipe. Grey's parents helped them out of the sludge pool. Then his dad quickly sealed the hatch before the water could flood the laboratory.

Grey's mom put a splint on Hamlin's arm. Then she sent Grey to the storage closet to change into a spare jumpsuit.

7 – Growing Closer

When Grey came back, the Penguins were dancing for Miranda and Lloyd. Hamlin sat quietly by himself.

"What happened to the station?" Grey asked, giving his dad a big hug.

"A large chunk of ice broke loose above us," Dad explained. "While ice floats, drilling equipment does not. A large tractor sank like a brick and crashed into the colony, rupturing the hull and disabling the submarine bay."

"So we're stuck in this lab until they fix the leak?" Lloyd said.

"It's better than a sewage pipe," Miranda replied.

Mom laughed. "Rescue Patrol should reach us in a few hours," she said. "We'll be fine until then."

Grey sat next to Hamlin.

"Thanks for saving me," Hamlin mumbled. Grey nodded.

"I never knew you had a garden here," Hamlin said. "My mom and I used to grow vegetables on the surface."

"You should stop by after your arm heals," Grey suggested. "We can always use help pulling weeds."

"Pulling weeds?" Hamlin said. "That's a dirty job."

Grey laughed. "Yeah, but somebody's gotta do it."

Going Deeper

Behind the Scenes

Waste Deep was written for the July 2016 issue of Clubhouse magazine. The main character and three penguins each have special names borrowed from my kids' middle names or nicknames; Grey, Waves, Grace, and Mae Mae.

The family's last name is Wikk, which is the same as the Wikks in The Quest for Truth, and yes these Wikks are ancestors to the ones in The Quest for Truth. But no, they won't meet; they are separated by thousands of years.

But as the story explains, the Earth (known in The Quest for Truth as Ursprung) is falling apart. Humans haven't been good stewards of what God gave us.

Overpopulation and pollution lead to famine and drought which resulted in blame and persecution and then war. It was then the Ark was built as a way to escape the Earth that was dying.

But this story takes place before, this story takes place when some still had hope. And today we still have hope that we can change our world and protect it for future generations.

BIBLICAL APPLICATION

Psalm 24:1 says, "The earth is the Lord's, and all it contains." Psalm 104:5a says, "He established the earth upon its foundation." Genesis 1:26 says, "Then God said, 'Let us make man in Our image according to Our likeness, and let them rule over the fish of the sea and over the birds of the sky and over the cattle and over all the Earth, and over every creeping thing that creeps on the earth.'" God has made the world, and He has put us in charge of it. Recycling and reducing waste is everyone's duty.

Science Experiment

Now gather your family and try this experiment together. By the end, you'll learn how different types of materials decompose at different rates. It's similar to the applications the Wikk family were using in their undersea laboratory.

Materials Needed:

1. 2 pieces of a vegetable or fruit (tomato or green pepper)
2. 1 plastic sandwich bag
3. 2 Mason jars
4. Soil

Method:

First, fill your two Mason jars with the same amount of soil (3/4ths full.)

Next, wrap one piece of green pepper in the sandwich bag and bury it in one of the Mason jars.

Place the other piece of pepper in a Mason jar containing soil without a sandwich bag wrapped around it.

The experiment will run for 7 days. Every 24 hours check the pieces of green pepper and make notes and draw pictures of the changes and differences you discover.

Before you start to come up with a family hypothesis to what will happen during the experiment. For example, which piece of green pepper will decompose more quickly? Will the soil change as a result of the added piece of green pepper?

Results:

At the end of the seven days write down the condition of the two pieces of green pepper. Compare them to each other. Now as a family discuss the week of observations and the final results.

Take it to the next level:

If your family's curiosity allows, extend the experiment to two or three weeks. At week two, examine the green pepper and note differences, then repeat activity at week three.

Another way to extend the project is to try a variety of foods. Bread and banana peel will decay differently than a green pepper will. Use the same format to compare decay across a variety of foods.

The Science:

Fruits and vegetables start to decay if left for a period of time. Microorganisms in the soil feed on the fruit or vegetable and break it down.

Bacteria don't like to feed on plastic, so materials like plastic take a longer time to degrade than organic materials like fruit or vegetables. Plastic can be broken down by UV light, a process called photodegradation, however, plastic dumped in a landfill often doesn't get exposed to much sunlight. Plastic in the ocean breaks down faster, but the problem with plastic is that it releases chemicals into the water which then build up in the food chain and can poison marine life.

Discussion Questions

I hope these questions will assist you, your family, and your friends in reflecting on this story. Take some time and write out your answers before you discuss. You can also share your answers with others @ BrockEastman.com.

1. What do you think it would be like to live under the ocean?

2. Grey has three penguins in the story that were sort of like pets. If you could choose any animal as a pet, what would it be?

3. What are at least two things Grey might be afraid of in this story?

4. Would you risk your life for someone who isn't kind to you? Why or why not?

5. Would you be ready to take on a dirty job if God asked you to?

Brock Eastman Book Checklist

- [ ] Taken
- [ ] Risk
- [ ] Unleash
- [ ] Tangle
- [ ] Hope
- [ ] Coming Storm
- [ ] Truthful test
- [ ] Waste Deep
- [ ] Wasted Wood
- [ ] HowlSage
- [ ] BlizzardSage
- [ ] CrimsonSage
- [ ] Rainbow Hippo
- [ ] Happy Hippo
- [ ] Count Hippo, Count
- [ ] Alpha Hippo
- [ ] Nebula Chronicles: Endeavor
- [ ] Nebula Chronicles: Velocity

For the most current list visit BrockEasmtnan.com

ABOUT THE AUTHOR

Brock Eastman lives in Colorado with his wife, four children, two cats. And no penguins, though his daughter Waverly does have a stuffed pink penguin that she takes everywhere.

Brock is the author of The Quest for Truth and Sages of Darkness series and writes for The Imagination Station series. He's been a producer for Adventures in Odyssey and works for Compassion International.

He enjoys getting letters and artwork from fans. You can contact him and keep track of what Brock is working on @ BrockEastman.com

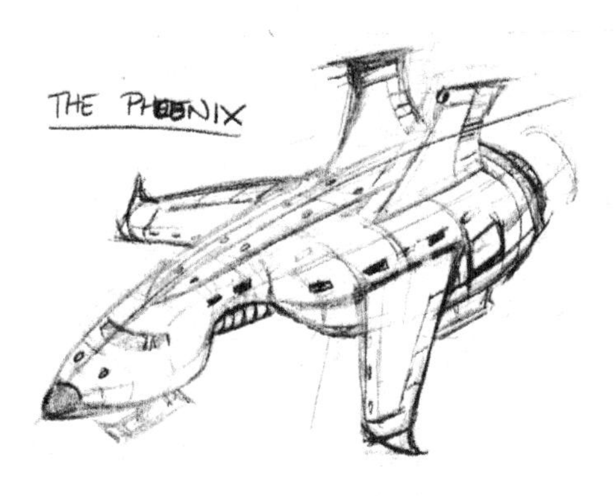

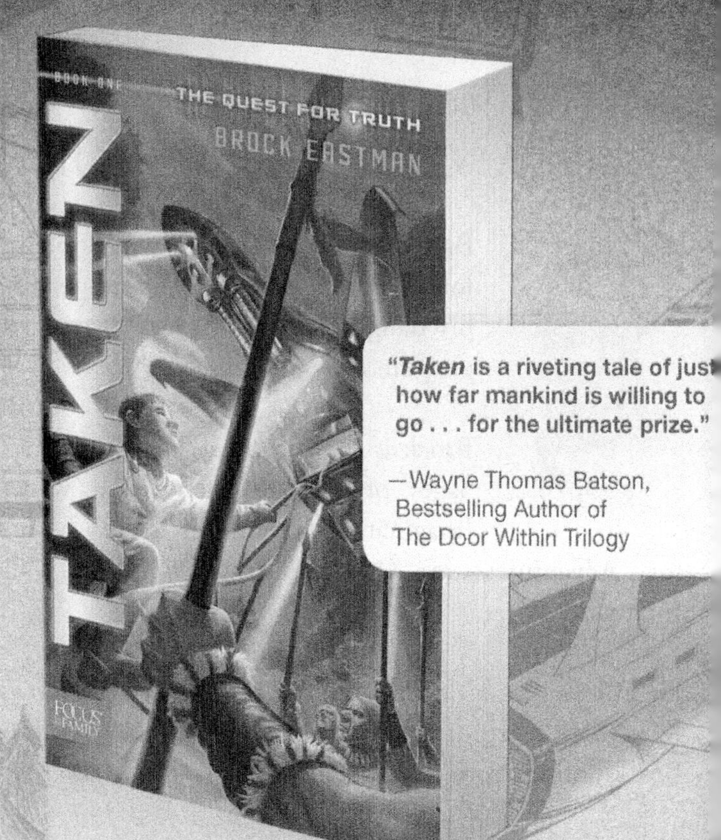
BOOK ONE
THE QUEST FOR TRUTH
BROCK EASTMAN
TAKEN
"*Taken* is a riveting tale of just how far mankind is willing to go . . . for the ultimate prize."
—Wayne Thomas Batson, Bestselling Author of The Door Within Trilogy

CPSIA information can be obtained
at www.ICGtesting.com
Printed in the USA
BVOW09s1646041217
501906BV00017B/805/P